THE DUKE'S SURPRISE VISITOR

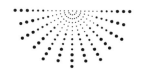

CHARITY MCCOLL

PUREREAD.COM

CONTENTS

1

IN SEARCH OF THE ONE

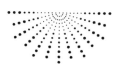

"Anthony."

"Yes, my lord?"

"Have someone saddle a horse for me, I've got to go round and visit my tenants," Lord Abel Wickham told his valet.

"As you please, your grace."

"Good. And ask Oliver to come up here and see me. That young pup has overstretched his allowance and the store owners and his other creditors are becoming a nuisance. They won't give me a moment's peace because my cousin's credit is a mess."

"Very well, your grace."

Once the valet had left, Abel sat at his writing desk and ran a hand through his thick dark hair. He knew that he was handsome and one of the most sought after men in England, but he also knew that he carried the weight of his duchy on his shoulders. Having become duke at the tender age of twenty two, he'd made a lot of mistakes along the way but thank God for faithful servants.

The men and women who had served his parents had showed him loyalty and now eight years later, the Duchy of Nottingham was one of the most stable in the whole of England. Besides that, his estate was very prosperous and self supporting, thanks to the good ideas of his estate manager.

There was a brief knock at his door before the person put their head in. "Come in, Oliver," Abel was older than his cousin by four years.

Their fathers were brothers, with Abel's being the older one by four years and had been the duke. His uncle, William had been a very loyal assistant and that was the reason Abel had taken Oliver in when his father died.

"You wanted to see me?" Oliver was never one to stand still, so he moved to the dressing table and picked up a pair of cufflinks. "These look really expensive, I bet they can pay the annual salary of two British soldiers fighting Napoleon in Europe."

Abel ignored the snide remark. He was used to his cousin making all kinds of comments about his clothes and accessories. In any case, he worked hard for whatever he possessed, unlike Oliver who expected to be spoon fed.

"It's good to see you looking good, dear cousin."

"Well, what else would I be?" Oliver's tone was sarcastic, "Seeing as I'm at the mercy of my relatives who feed me very well."

"If you're not contented with your lot, why don't you enlist in the army and earn a salary?" Abel was tired of pampering his selfish cousin who did nothing more than complain, gamble and spend money that he hadn't earned. "The Duke of Wellington still needs men out there to help fight Napoleon."

"Why don't you join the army," Oliver mocked. "No, wait. Far be it for the Royal Duke of Nottingham to be found in the trenches alongside the commoners."

Abel thought about making an unkind remark but then realised that it was exactly what Oliver wanted, for them to exchange words. "Whatever you feel about me, Oliver, I'm still your cousin and the duke. I don't expect you to respect me but it wouldn't hurt for you to be a less condescending."

Oliver bowed in mock homage. "Forgive your humble servant, your grace." He straightened out. "What did you want me for?"

"These debts of yours," Abel pushed a pile of promissory notes at his cousin. "You seem to owe everyone and it's getting rather uncomfortable for me when I meet your creditors."

"If you would only increase my allowance, I wouldn't have to get so desperate and end up in debt."

"Increasing your allowance isn't the option I'll go with now. You need to limit your expenditure to only the things you need, not those that you desire or want."

"What's the difference? If I am to impress some girl into becoming my wife, don't I have to look like a baron?"

"Your baronetcy would flourish if only you put your heart into sorting out your estate. You have no excuse for not doing well, Oliver. Uncle William was very hard working..."

"Yes, yes, so you keep telling me. Get off my back, Abel. This is my life and I don't want you or anyone else telling me how to run it.

I've just about had enough of all that from you. You see me as an irresponsible young man but you haven't had to work with what I have. Now, if there's nothing else you need me for, I have to be going. Luke is waiting for me so we can go and check out some race horses that he'd like to buy."

And just like that, Oliver exited the room. Abel's look was troubled as he studied the closed door. His cousin seemed to be goading him more and more these days. Nothing he said was ever followed and short of cutting him off the estate, there wasn't much he could do. Besides, he'd promised his uncle that he would always take care of his cousin. But Oliver was getting out of hand and something needed to be done before he crossed a line from which he couldn't return.

With a sigh, Abel rang the bell for his valet. "Is the horse ready for me?"

"Yes, your grace. I was waiting for you to finish with your cousin," Anthony's voice was disapproving. Even without being told, Abel knew that the elderly man strongly disapproved of Oliver. But he was too polite to say anything, though he never went out of his way to do anything he didn't have to for the young man.

"Would you keep an eye on Oliver for me please? I'm getting rather concerned because Lord Luke Froth isn't the kind of company I want him keeping. For one, Luke is lazy and a spendthrift. He's also heavily in debt but has his father's estate to bail him out. Oliver on the other hand, has to rely on my goodwill and I'm afraid the grace to continue supporting him is long running out.

"Cut him loose, is what I would do," Anthony said, then remembered who he was addressing. "Pardon me, your grace."

"It's alright, but just keep me informed about what my cousin is up to."

"Yes, your grace."

2
ABUNDANT GRACE

Matilda Johnson heard one of her fellow wardens shouting at someone down the corridor and sighed. Even without being told, she knew who the culprit was. Sephora Oswald was at it again. What had the girl done this time, she wondered.

"Sephora Oswald, if you don't come here this instant, I'll box those ears till they're black and blue."

"I didn't do it," Sephora shouted back. She was never one to back down from a fight whether between her and the other children or even with the wardens. When she felt she was right, nothing could make her change her mind. "You're always picking on me and yet I told you that I didn't do it."

Tilda knew that if she didn't step out of her room and into the fight, it would turn ugly. "Sephora, what's going on here? What have I told you about being disrespectful to your superiors?"

"Miss Johnson, it wasn't me to spilled the water all over the common room. I've tried to tell Miss Ellison that but she won't listen to me."

"This girl is rude and disrespectful and if you don't do something about her, I'll ask the senior warden to get her out of this place. She deserves to be in a public orphanage, not one sponsored by the church. Good thing I'm not your mother."

"Good. Because I'd rather be an orphan than be your daughter," Sephora retorted and Tilda felt that things had gone on long enough.

"Sephora, get into my room at once."

"But..."

"I said now," Tilda's face and voice brooked no nonsense. "I'll deal with you later." She waited until the sixteen year old had entered the room before turning to her colleague. "I'm really sorry about this, Lydia. Please forgive Sephora, she's just a child."

"That girl is old enough to be someone's wife and I don't know why we still keep her here. She's rude, obnoxious and likes fighting everyone. Why did we ever take her in?"

"Please don't say that about a child who needed us. Sephora has never gotten over the death of her parents and we need to help her through till she's ready."

"It's been what, six years now since she was brought here. Why won't she just fit in with the rest of the children?"

"No amount of time can make up for the loss of a parent, especially in Sephora's case. She was an only child and beloved of her parents. Their deaths were quite untimely and unfortunate and she still can't get over the fact that she'll never go home."

"We deal with children who've been through worse. It doesn't help that you treat that girl like a princess. You yourself were brought up in this orphanage, you didn't you turn out bad like this one."

Tilda didn't want to get into an argument with her colleague.

"I'll talk to Sephora and see that she comes to make an apology to you." Lydia snorted. "She's really a good child, just confused and sad."

"You're only two years older than her and yet one would think you're her mother. Don't overindulge her. Besides, Mrs. Worth said she was considering taking Sephora to the Juvenile Delinquency Centre which is where she'll fit right in."

"What?" As if realising that she'd said too much, Lydia turned and fled, leaving Tilda staring at her fast retreating back. How could they have discussed such a serious issue without informing her? With a sigh, she opened her door and found Sephora seated demurely at her table.

"What were you doing?" She looked at the girl suspiciously. Upon immediate view, nothing looked out of place. But Tilda had long learned that Sephora wasn't to be trusted.

"Nothing, Miss Johnson.:

"You know I don't like it when you call me that," Tilda's keen eye took in the fact that Sephora looked a little uncomfortable. "What did you touch, and if you say nothing, I'll box your ears." It was an empty threat and she knew it as did Sephora.

"I'm sorry, Tilda, but I saw your journal lying open on the table," she pointed at the now closed journal. "I just couldn't resist."

"That's invading my privacy. How many times have I told you that it's disrespectful to touch other people's things without permission?"

"I'm sorry."

"And so should you be. Now, go and find Miss Ellison and apologise to her immediately. Maybe as they say, I've been too gentle with you and you're my direct responsibility. Sephora, you're growing up and it's time that you learned how to be more responsible and less of a problem to everyone."

"I'll go now," Sephora looked hurt and Tilda regretted her words.

"Sephora..."

But the girl was gone and she sat down on her bed. It was true that she was directly responsible for the girl. Sephora had come to the orphanage when she was only ten and

Tilda was twelve. From the moment she saw the sad little girl, she'd taken her under her wings. Being the darling of the orphanage at the time, Tilda had slightly better privileges than the rest and that meant Sephora benefitted too. Over the years, Tilda had covered for her charge so many times but perhaps it was time to stop. She acknowledged that she wasn't doing the girl any good but she just couldn't let the poor child get into trouble.

Her hands automatically reached for the journal in which she often penned her deepest desires. Before being interrupted by the quarrel, she'd been writing about finding love.

"Some ancient writers call it the illusion of mankind, while others hail love as the force that makes the world a better place for all of us. What is this love, and how does someone know when they find it? How will I know when I meet the man who is supposed to make my heart race, my palms sweat and butterflies fill my stomach? Will he be a common man, labouring hard to earn a living, or

will he be a nobleman who's never had to do a day's work?

Can anyone control who they fall in love with, or should I just accept it as inevitable when it comes?"

She tried to write some more but her thoughts kept returning to the troubled young girl who'd left her room just a few minutes ago. What was she going to do about Sephora so the child wouldn't be thrown out of the orphanage? Tilda missed the days when the walls of the orphanage had resounded with the laughter of little happy children, days when wardens did all they could for their charges. These days, it was mostly about pleasing sponsors and donors at the expense of the children. Tilda knew that the senior warden was serious about kicking Sephora out because it had happened to a little fifteen year old child just months before. The girl had found herself in the family way and when asked who was responsible, had mentioned the name of a donor. The man in question was loving and caring, or so everyone had thought, until that moment.

Had it been in days past, the senior warden who was there at the time would have done all she could to ensure that the girl and her baby were taken care of, while the man was made to pay for his misdemeanours. Unfortunately, however, Mrs. Worth had claimed that the poor girl was a liar and kicked her out of the home. Sephora tried to follow up and find out where she could be, asking for help from the Bow Street Runners. That's when she'd come into contact with a young man named Mark Blaze, and who seemed to want more than just friendship from her. Unfortunately, she saw him as a kind older brother and nothing more.

By the time Mark found Clara, it was too late. Distraught and desperate, she'd tried to rid herself of the pregnancy but lost her life instead. From then on, Tilda tried her best to do all she could for the especially troubled children, Sephora included. She knew that sending the child to a Juvenile Delinquency

Centre was the same as sending her out on the streets. No one really cared and the girls were subjected to all manner of horrors, if stories that emerged from that place were to be believed. No one took responsibility for their actions and she prayed that she would reach out to Sephora and help before things really got out of hand.

Someone was shaking her and Tilda wanted to slap the hand away. "Miss Johnson, please wake up."

"What is it?" She opened her eyes to find three girls of about fifteen years old standing in her room. "How did you get into my room I had the door locked?" Her eyes went to the door which seemed to be locked and even bolted from the inside. "Anna, talk now or you'll be in a lot of trouble."

"We're sorry, Miss Johnson. We tried to knock on the door but you wouldn't open so Mary climbed up the trellis and entered through the window. She opened the door for us but we've bolted it again."

"That was a foolish and dangerous thing to do, Mary. What if you'd fallen and broken your leg or arm?"

"I know how to climb trees and walls, Miss Johnson," Mary replied indignantly. "I didn't fall."

"Yes, you didn't fall. Now that you're in my room what seems to be the problem?"

"Miss Johnson, Sephora is gone."

"Gone where?"

"We don't know," Anna said. "We just realised that we hadn't seen her before dinner and thought she was sulking because of quarrelling with Miss Lydia. But when we went to bed, she didn't come to the dormitory so we thought she might be here with you."

"You know that it's an offence for any of you to be out of the dorm at this time," Tilda pulled her gown on. "Did she take anything with her?"

"We don't know," this from Mary. "You know that none of us ever touch her stuff, or she'll kill us."

"Harsh words to use on your dorm mate. Shall we go and see what she took then? It might make us know where she at, or she could just have gone to the church roof like she likes to do, so she can paint the stars."

"We checked but she's not there."

"Fine, Anna. Let's go find your friend."

Tilda decided to first inform Rebecca Worth, the senior warden because a child missing from the orphanage could create all manner of problems.

"That child is stubborn and a troublemaker," Rebecca said. "I'm not about to use any of the orphanage's resources to search for that delinquent. She often threatened to run away and has finally done it. Good thing none of us were involved and being of age, she probably decided to spare us all the trouble. I was about to kick her out anyway."

Tilda didn't make any comment at her superior's unkind words but just thanked her and motioned for the three girls to follow her. She would find Sephora, even if it took her the whole night.

Search as they did, the four of them failed to find Sephora. Tilda finally ended up in the dorm and went through the girl's things. Two things alerted her to the fact that if Sephora had indeed left the orphanage, she hadn't done so willingly. The child could never go anywhere without her locket. She'd told Tilda years ago, that it was given to her by her parents for her tenth birthday, just weeks before they died. In it were miniature pictures of her father and mother, and Sephora never took the locket off unless she was going to take a bath.

Because of her love of painting, Tilda had bought her a beautiful sketch book and she'd only done two sketches so far. That was the second thing she wouldn't have left the orphanage without. Something had happened to the child.

"I don't think Sephora ran away," she told the three girls. "Someone must have taken her out of this place by force. Could you please find out who she's been talking to lately? Probably a staff member, but be very discreet."

"Yes, Miss. Johnson."

3

TO THE RESCUE

"**A**ccording to my sources, the girl ended up here," Mark Blaze pointed at some dark buildings on the waterfront. Tilda recognised them as abandoned warehouses and her heart sank. Just like she'd guessed, Sephora hadn't run away but had been taken out of the orphanage by one of the staff members who had also stopped coming to work.

Brenda Sunderland, according to the other children, had become quite close with Sephora and on the day the child disappeared, had promised to take her to her parents' grave and then buy her a birthday cake. When Tilda told Mark all this, he went over to the housing unit where Brenda lived but was informed that she had left the day before. And yes, she had a young girl of about sixteen with her. The girl looked happy enough though the neighbours couldn't be sure.

"What could she possibly be doing in a place like this," Tilda whispered. Mark had told her to be very quiet because this area was dangerous. It was well known for illegal activities like smuggling and even he and his colleagues were quite careful whenever they had to come to the old Liverpool docks.

"One thing is clear, if the child was brought here, then she's probably on a ship to America by now," Mark said and Tilda wanted to cry out. "In which case all we can do is report her as missing but I won't hold my breath at her being found. Girls who are put on slave ships and sent out to be sold to people in America and other colonies are rarely found. All we can do is pray that whoever buys her will be kind to her."

But Tilda refused to believe that it was all over for her charge. She'd also failed Sephora by being very harsh with her a few days ago. She was sure that was the reason that the child had been enticed by the other warden. Tilda had never liked Brenda much. They were both wardens but she refused to take up the quarters that all other wardens had in the orphanage. Instead, she lived in a housing unit and always seemed to have money. They were paid the same wages but Brenda always had money to lend her colleagues, with interest of course.

Now a picture began forming in Tilda's mind. What if Brenda was involved in the selling of young girls from the orphanage? It was a weakness that anyone could exploit since no one ever made a follow up of the girls once they turned eighteen and were put out of the orphanage to make room for more children.

Tilda had been lucky because she got interested in working for the institution and had been offered a job there for about a year now. That was because they were short of wardens and she was seventeen when she got the job.

"What are you thinking?" Mark asked Tilda.

"Would it be possible to search all the buildings?"

"Waste of time, Miss Johnson."

"I know that, but let's just do it. We might find something that will lead us to knowing what happened to Sephora."

"It's a long shot in the dark but I'll do it, and only because it's you. I don't want you getting into any trouble so I'll insist on you staying at an inn. Wait for me to come to you and under no circumstances are you to try and follow me. Like I said, these old warehouses harbour all manner of vermin of the human kind and for a woman, it could be very dangerous."

"Thank you, Mark," Tilda held his hands. "Please hurry. I'll not leave the inn until you return."

Mark returned nearly three hours later. He looked excited. "It may be something or it may be nothing, but please come with me."

"Where?"

"To the docks. I was about to give up my search when I peeked into one of the warehouses and saw two girls. I didn't want to alert them to my presence so I came to get you. They might know something about the girl that you seek."

"Let's go."

"Who are you?" A voice emerged from the darkness and Tilda smiled.

"Sephora, come out. It's just me."

"Miss Johnson?" The child emerged from behind some old crates and when she saw Tilda, rushed and fell into her arms. "I'm sorry, I didn't run away, Miss Johnson."

"I know that, and please keep your voice down. We're in a very dangerous place right now. Are you alone?"

"No, I was taking care of another girl who was left here when we were put on the ship."

'You were put on a ship?" Tilda asked, quite horrified.

"Yes, but I pretended to be very ill and they carried me back here to die."

"Whos' they?"

"Some men who were taking us on the ship. Miss Johnson, I promise I didn't run away," Sephora was crying. "Miss Sunderland told me that since it was nearly my birthday, she would take me to visit my parents' graves and then buy me a dress and a birthday cake."

27

"What then happened?"

"She gave me over to some people who brought me here," When she got into the carriage that Miss Sunderland had hired, she soon realised that she was being abducted. They travelled for three days and nights until they got to Liverpool and then she was brought to this warehouse, where she found a number of girls her age. All had either been forcefully taken away from their families or were enticed with the promise of a better life and only realised the trouble they were in once they got to Liverpool. Sephora had found out that they were to be taken to America as Mail Order Brides against their will and consent. There were about forty girls in all and five of them fell seriously ill and died. The young girl with her was Kathleen Crammer and when she also fell ill, the slave traders abandoned her. Sephora and the others had been taken to a ship but she managed to escape and returned to help Kathleen.

"I couldn't just leave Kate here alone because she was going to die."

"You're a good girl, Sephora. And I'm sorry that I didn't realise it before."

Mark took them to a small but very private inn. "This is one of the safest places you can be, but don't go out very early in the morning or at night. These are dangerous times and with the slave trading booming, any young woman is an easy target. Those criminals usually target young ladies and girls who are alone. Be very careful."

"We will," Tilda promised. She couldn't stay away from her work for too long but these girls were her responsibility and as soon as Kathleen was better, they would find her family. She would take Sephora back to the orphanage and plead her case. As for Brenda Sunderland, Mark promised to find and take stern action against her.

"Thank you so much for what you did for Sephora," Tilda told him. "May God bless you."

"I'll come looking for you when you're back in London."

"I'd like that very much."

4
A NEW LIFE

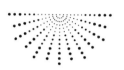

Lord Abel Wickham had just returned from London and was resting in his chambers when he was informed that there were some young women to see him. Thinking it was the usual group of girls who liked to hang around Oliver and making a nuisance of themselves, he left his bedroom with one purpose in mind. To get them off his estate as fast as he could.

It was two days to Christmas and he was supposed to be hosting a party that could either end in a single day or stretch for days, depending on the crowd. He admitted that he was getting too old for some of these wild parties as Gerald Brinks his butler liked to call them. What made him angry was that nearly half of his staff were down with influenza and couldn't work at all. The upside was that only a skeletal staff were full time residents at the manor. The rest lived in quarters assigned to them all over the estate so that was a blessing, else they would all be ill. Having to cater for a large group of his friends who would begin arriving at any time was going to be a challenge and he would have to get some women from the village to help out. What a mess! Had Anthony been here, he would have known exactly who to bring to help at the manor. But he was gone forever and that had been a great blow to Abel.

He missed Anthony, who'd fallen ill and passed away just days ago. Losing the old man had made him realise that he'd come to depend on him so much. At the moment, he was in the process of finding himself a new valet but wondered if anyone would be able to put up with his peculiarities like Anthony had done.

Gerald hadn't let the women into the house and when Abel stepped out onto the front landing and saw them, wondered who they were. They looked so weary, like they'd been travelling for a long time. And it was quite cold outside, having snowed heavily the night before.

"Who are you and what do you want?"

"Your grace," the oldest one curtsied. "My name is Matilda Johnson, this is Sephora Oswald and this is Kathleen Crammer."

"How may I help you?"

"Your grace, I work as a warden at St. Phillip's Children's Orphanage in London. A few days ago, Sephora here was abducted by some people who took her to Liverpool, intending to get her on a boat to America." Abel made a sound of dismay. One of the bills that he was fighting to push through in parliament was bringing stern measures against all those involved in human trafficking. No young lady was safe from the traffickers.

"Go on."

"With the help of a friend who is a Bow Street Runner, we found Sephora but she wasn't alone. She informed us that in the group, she'd met Kathleen here, who had also been sold to those dealers. Kathleen was very ill and nearly died, so we nursed her for about three days. When she was finally able to speak, she told us that she had been on her way to Nottingham to find her uncle, her mother's brother. She lost her purse to a pickpocket and when she asked a motherly looking woman for help, found herself in a carriage. That was the last thing she remembered until she woke up in the warehouse."

"I'm very sorry for your troubles, perhaps the young lady's uncle is known to me. I could find out who it is." Abel wondered why the three women were looking at him strangely. "Did I say something wrong?"

Tilda turned to Kathleen. "Go on and tell him everything."

"Your grace," Kathleen curtsied. "Just before my mama died, she told me to come to Nottingham and find my uncle who she was sure would help me."

"Good, now what's his name so I can send someone to bring him here?"

"It's you, your grace."

Abel thought he hadn't heard right. "What do you mean me?"

"Aren't you Abel Wickham?"

"That I am, but I don't have a sister, living or dead. You must have gotten the name wrong and are quite mistaken."

"I know what mama told me," Kathleen was nearly in tears and Tilda knew she had to take control of the situation.

"Your grace, we've come a long way and are really tired. Perhaps if you asked someone, they might tell you that Kathleen is speaking the truth."

"As the head of this family, I would know if there were any missing children from the lineage. So far, I haven't heard of any so I'm quite sorry."

Abel wanted to really help the three women because related to him or not, Kate Crammer looked like his wayward cousin, Tamara. He was glad she was in Paris doing something but he had no idea what, and didn't really care. Between Tamara and Oliver, they were making him age very fast. Still, this child might be the baseborn child of one of his relatives and he needed time to find out which one it was. There was only one way to find out for sure.

"I hope you don't mind, but I'd like to offer you some temporary work." He had another selfish reason for wanting to keep the three women around him. Matilda Johnson had touched his heart in a way that no other woman had. While he couldn't just invite her to live in his house without having to explain her presence to so many people, having her there as a housekeeper would give him time to know what to do.

"Why?" Kate demanded, dashing her tears away. "It's obvious you don't want us here so why would you want us to work in your house?"

Tilda threw Abel an apologetic glance and then pulled the two girls aside. "Kate, I know it hurts that you're not being recognized as a child of this family but you have got to understand something."

"What?"

"If this had been you and someone just walked up to your house and claimed that they were your dead sister's child, and to your knowledge you don't have one, what would you do?"

"Invite them in and find out the truth."

"Don't you think that's what your uncle is trying to do? As a duke, he has to protect himself, his family and this estate. If you ask me, he wants to keep us here so he can find out if you're really genuine."

Sephora laughed softly. "Miss Johnson always sees the good in people, Kate. Don't bother arguing with her," this was said when Kate tried to open her mouth.

"In any case," Tilda said, "This is one way that we can find out from the other servants whether they know anything about your mother. We can't just dismiss his offer like that."

"I just don't like it."

"You don't have to like the circumstances, Kate, but consider it a necessary evil for you to find out the truth."

"Alright then."

"Good. Now, I'm going back over there to speak to the duke. Keep your mouth shut and let's enter the manor. The truth is somewhere within these walls and our being diligent will help. You know how servants learn a lot of things. Let's hold on to that and we shall eventually find the truth."

"Thank you, Miss Johnson."

Once Tilda was sure the girls wouldn't bring up any more arguments, she went back to Abel, who was waiting somewhat impatiently. "Your grace, we accept your offer."

Abel wanted to clap his hands but his position wouldn't allow him. It wouldn't do for anyone to know how happy he was that Matilda and the other ladies were staying.

"Very well then, if you go round the back, Gerald will show you what needs to be done. I'll let him know that you're coming to him." He waited until they were on their way to the backyard before entering the house. "Gerald."

"Your grace," the man gave a slight bow.

"I've temporarily hired those three ladies to help with catering for the festivities. See that they're not bothered by anyone and you know who I mean."

"Have no fear, your grace. Your cousin hasn't been home for the past three days though I know that he's bound to show up when the guests start arriving."

"Miss Johnson looks mature enough to handle herself, it's the other two that I'm worried about."

"I'll be on the lookout for any problems."

"Thank you."

5
SINISTER HAPPENINGS

Tilda had never worked so hard in her life before, but this was an interesting job to say the least. Lord Abel's house was beautiful and she found out from one of the male servants that his mother had loved art and collected rare pieces. The former duke had indulged his young wife and all the pieces around the sprawling mansion were originals.

She also tried to find out more about the family line but two of the servants she spoke with informed her that they'd only come to work for the family a few years before.

"I don't think we're getting anywhere," Kate told her on Christmas Eve's Day.

"Child, we've only been here a day and a half and spoken to a few of the servants. It's a pity the rest are indisposed, but just calm down. Once the festivities are over, I'm sure we'll find someone who will give us more information. Meanwhile, I need those pots and pans well cleaned.

"Yes, Miss Johnson."

Sephora came into the kitchen looking really annoyed. "These people are a real nuisance," she complained. "It's do this, do that, bring me this, take this over there," she made a sound of disgust. "Who do they think they're talking to like that?

Tilda hid a smile. From when she was younger, Sephora had declared that she would never be anyone's servant for fear of harming her masters should they cross her.

"Sephora, this is a temporary post and besides, the money is good. Once we're done with the duke and his guests, we'll have some good money."

"I'm not complaining about the money," Sephora said with a twinkle in her eyes. "It's what I have to do to get it that's the problem."

"Like I've always told you, nothing good comes easily. In any case, we're here because we want to help Kate and her uncle."

"Lord Wickham doesn't seem to want to have anything to do with me."

"Kate, my dear, as I was telling you, we've only been here for a very short time. Right now, the duke has guests from all over and is concentrating on them. Be patient, child, if we have to get to the bottom of all this, you're going to need to stop worrying and complaining."

"Miss Johnson?"

"Yes, Sephora?"

"Do you like the duke?"

"Your question is quite odd and need I ask why?"

"Because he strikes me as being a good man. Maybe a little confused and all but with a good heart."

Tilda was surprised at Sephora's observation for that was the same one she had of the duke. "Why would you say that?"

"I overheard two of the servants saying that he takes good care of those who work for him, and also the tenants on his estate. His people like him very much."

"That's nice, but what does any of it have to do with me liking Kate's uncle?"

"What if you and the duke fell in love?" Sephora had a dreamy expression on her face. "Then we could get to live here forever and won't have to go back to that accursed orphanage. You will become the duchess, just fancy that, Miss Johnson."

"Well Sephora, fancy me boxing your ears because of your fantasies. Get your head out of the clouds, child, and help us with laying the table for dinner. This isn't the time to go daydreaming and there's so much that needs to be done."

"Yes, Miss Johnson."

But even as they worked to lay out dinner for the duke and his guests, Tilda couldn't help thinking about the man in whose house they were. He was really odd, that she had to admit. They'd been in the house only a day and a half but it felt like longer. Lord Wickham had come to the kitchen a number of times on the pretext of checking on the progress of the meals for his guests. Somehow, Tilda felt that there was more but she didn't know what. Each time he made sure that she was alone in the kitchen.

At that precise moment, Lord Wickham was thinking about the woman down below in his kitchen. He was preparing himself for the Christmas Eve dinner and not for the first time wished he hadn't invited so many people. There was plenty of food of course, and Matilda Johnson had proved to him that she could handle whatever came to her. But he realised that he'd been getting quite weary of too much entertainment for some time now. It was time for him to settle down. Watching Tilda as she got everything ready made him glad that he'd asked her to work for him. She was calm and level headed and even Gerald seemed to think that she was a special woman.

"It isn't everyday that a person walks into the manor and takes over. Reminds me of your Mama," Gerald had commented earlier that day. "Everything is in capable hands, your grace."

The comment pleased Abel but he didn't want his servant to immediately know why. "What about the other servants, what do they think?"

"We're just happy not to have to do the cooking. Besides, they're practically eating out of Miss Johnson's hand. She has a way of getting people to do things for her that is really interesting. She asks in the most apologetic and polite way, much like..."

"Yes, yes, like Mama used to do," Abel smiled. "Let's just make sure all is ready for the guests."

"You can be sure that the table will have all you need, and then some."

As he fixed his cravat, Abel wondered how he was going to broach the subject of marriage to Matilda Johnson. She also looked capable of handling his wayward relatives and goodness knows he needed a wife who wouldn't be turned into a doormat. The young lady could hold her own. He needed a good wife and she fit the post perfectly. The only question was, how was he going to get her to accept his suit?

If Gerald was to be believed, dinner was a huge success and everyone seemed very happy. Tilda was happy too because the duke had given them an early night off. Once they'd served all the food into the large dishes, he'd sent Gerald to tell her that they could go to bed early.

"You'll be catering for tomorrow's breakfast and lunch and I need you to be well rested," was the message Gerald had brought.

She lay in the dark listening to whatever was going on upstairs. It was all because of Kate that she'd agreed to take on this job, but it wasn't something she wanted to do more than was necessary. Being a cook in a duke's home was hard work. They had cooked until she felt that her nose couldn't tell the difference between the various dishes. So far, no one had complained about the food and she was just glad there were only twenty to thirty guests staying at the manor. The rest were coming in from around and those really weren't her problem.

She had just begun to drift off when she thought she heard people talking. At first, Tilda thought the voices were coming from the kitchen. Her senses became alert and she listened keenly, and realised the sound was coming through the walls. She could tell that it was two men talking and the voices faded away. What made her pay attention was the fact that she thought she heard them mentioning the duke, and not in a nice way.

Curiosity got the better of her and she got out of the bed that she shared with the two younger ladies. They were fast asleep and she covered them. Poor lambs were so exhausted, having worked so hard. The fact that she'd heard voices through the walls meant that there was a secret passage and that meant a panel to access it. She'd read about how old manors and castles had secret passageways used in the days when a lot of smuggling went on. The passages also made it easy for families to escape from enemies should their homes be attacked.

So she felt along the walls of the room she and the girls were sleeping in, but didn't find anything. That left the second room which was also part of the servants' quarters. It didn't take her long to find the panel and she carefully opened it. The voices sounded some steps ahead of her and she waited. The last thing she wanted was to be discovered before she had gone very far. Slipping out, she crouched low in case any of the men decided to turn around. They stopped, opened a panel and went through it. She waited a few minutes and crept towards the place they had disappeared into. Their voices were loud, as if they didn't care who was listening. But Tilda knew it was because they felt confident that no one would hear their conversation above the din that was going on upstairs.

"It has to be done tonight because everyone is in high spirits," one of the men was saying. "Tomorrow will be too late."

"What if people ask where Abel is, what will we tell them?"

The first man laughed. "The lot upstairs are here only for the food, drink and fun. No one will care where their precious duke is and will just assume some filly spirited him off for the night."

"Are you really sure about this? If we get caught, can you imagine the kind of trouble we'll be in?"

"You worry too much, no one is going to catch us. But let's just be careful in any case."

Tilda felt that she'd heard enough and when the men's voices fell silent, she feared that they might be returning to the tunnel and so she hastened back to the servants' quarters. Her heart was pounding as she wondered who the two men were. Obviously, they knew this manor well, which meant that they'd lived here for a long time. Were they servants or relatives? She had to get to the duke and warn him before someone harmed him.

Abel wanted to wind up the party and get everyone going, but he'd invited them and so had to bear with the madness in his house. Deep within him, he knew that this was going to be the last merry party that would ever be thrown in this house. After this, any form of social gathering will be very formal and dignified. He was done with this wild side of his nature and he knew that a lot of it had to do with the young woman working as his cook.

He'd only known Matilda Johnson for two days, yet he couldn't stop thinking about her. He wondered what she thought of the partying and revelry and even felt slightly ashamed of himself. Something was changing within him and he found himself wanting to earn her approval.

That meant doing away with all the strong drinks that he was so used to, like the one in his hand which was giving him a headache. It was funny that no matter how much he drank, it never impaled his senses. Yet tonight, he'd only taken one drink but felt that his head was about to explode.

There was a soft knock at his study door. "Come in," he croaked and wondered whether the person had heard him or not. When the door opened, he was surprised to find Tilda standing there.

"Your grace," she stepped into the study and curtsied.

"Just the very person that I'd like to see," Abel wanted to rise to his feet but found that he didn't have the strength, which was very odd. "I don't feel so good."

"You don't look so good," Tilda stepped into the room, a frown on her face. The bright light from the beeswax candles that Gerald had lit earlier in the evening and the merry fire burning in the heath accentuated his sickly pallor. "You could be coming down with some ailment," she found herself saying and hoped he wouldn't reprimand her for daring to address him as an equal.

"Would you get.." his speech was becoming slurred and he blinked rapidly to dispel the darkness that was threatening to overcome him.

"May I get you some lemon, honey and hot water?" According to Tilda, that concoction was the cure for nearly all ailments and she'd used it a lot at the orphanage. "If it's the flu coming upon you, that should hold it at bay."

"Thank you," Abel placed his head on the desk. He was suddenly feeling so tired and just wanted to sleep.

"I'll be back shortly," Tilda promised as she rushed out of the room. She was glad that the duke was alright for the moment, and thought that he had probably imbibed too much. The revelling was as loud as ever and she winced as she walked in the shadows, careful to avoid the revellers who were walking all over the place. The last thing she wanted was to meet a drunk man and get into any kind of trouble. Besides, the duke needed her right now and the sooner she got him the drink, the better.

Abel felt a slight draught at his back and tried to lift his head. He could sense a presence in the room but couldn't see anyone.

"Who ......?" Was all he managed to get out before he felt a sharp blow to the back of his head.

Tilda hurried and prepared the drink, serving it in a tea pot and carried it to the duke's study. Apart from one or two servants, she met no one else along the corridors and just pushed the door in, in case the duke had already fallen asleep.

"Your grace, I..." the words died on her lips when she saw that the room was empty. Placing the tray on the table, she walked to the large desk and stood staring at the chair where she'd left the duke not more than ten minutes ago. He had probably gone to bed, she thought in disappointment. She had hoped to spend a minute or two with him as he took his lemon and honey, and it wasn't just because she wanted to find out if his heart was changing towards Kate. She liked the duke, very much and this would have been the perfect excuse to spend time with him. Tilda had no idea what she hoped to achieve, but she felt a sharp sense of loss.

As she turned to leave, the candle on the large desk flickered as if there was draught in the room and she frowned. As far as she could tell, the windows were all shut and there shouldn't be any air coming in. The candle flickered again and her eyes went to the panels behind the duke's desk. One seemed to be slightly uneven and she hurried over to take a closer look. It slid back as soon as she pressed it gently and something gleamed up at her from the floor.

Bending down, she saw that it was one of the duke's cufflinks and her mind finally took in that the duke hadn't left for his bed. She wanted to run up to his bedroom and find out if he was there, but something urged her to slip through the open panel and into the tunnel.

The tunnel was dimly lit but she managed to see that someone, most probably the duke, had been dragged along by more than one person. Her heart was pounding and she prayed that it wasn't too late to save the duke from the wicked men. What if they'd already killed him and were going to dispose of his body?

"Dear Lord, please don't let Abel be dead," she murmured as her feet seemed to find wings. When she'd been walking for nearly ten minutes, she heard a sound ahead and slowed down. The last thing she wanted was to walk right up to the men and reveal her presence

"You didn't tell me that this man was so heavy," one voice complained.

"Stop all that whining and help me get him out of here. We have to hurry so we can go back to the manor and ensure that our presence is conspicuous to everyone."

"Why? I'm tired and just want to go and sleep."

"Don't be such an idiot. Tomorrow when the constable finds Abel, he's going to question everyone and it's important that people remember seeing us at the stupid party. Otherwise, suspicion will fall on us."

"I hope you know what you're doing."

"I do. Now shut up and let's get out of here. These tunnels aren't the best place to be at this hour."

Tilda waited for them to move further away before she followed, careful to stay hidden in the shadows.

"Did you see that?"

"What now?"

"I thought I saw something or someone."

"You're beginning to get on my nerves now. Shut up and help me get this man out of here so we can return to whatever it is we were doing."

"But ...."

"Shut up."

Tilda took a deep breath and sighed in relief. She was going to have to be really careful or else she could get into a lot of trouble.

"Just a few feet and we're there," the harsh voice said. "Pull yourself together or you might give the game away."

Tilda felt a rush of cold and wished she had thought of putting on something warmer than her housecoat. It was too late now and the men ahead suddenly disappeared from view. Her heart pounded and she stopped, letting her eyes adjust to the darkness. Mercifully, it hadn't snowed but she was sure it wouldn't remain so for long. She had to find out where the men were taking the duke so she could save him before it was too late.

A twig snapped and she jumped, crouching low. Then she saw two dark figures ahead and followed again, but for a short distance this time.

"This is it. Let's leave him here for now and then we'll be back in the morning to finish off what we started. By the time anyone finds his body, we'll be in our beds and nursing hangovers like everyone else."

Tilda hid behind a tree wishing she could see clearly and know who the men were. But that would also give her position away and she crouched lower. A door creaked open and in a few minutes it shut again.

"Let's go back." The men passed so close to where she was hiding that if she had reached out a hand, might have touched them. She remained in that position for a while, just in case they returned, and also to give them plenty of time to be gone from the tunnels when she returned.

Once she was sure they weren't coming back, she made her way to the structure which she guessed to be a woodcutter's hut, and opened it. She stumbled across Abel's still form and cried out softly. "Your grace," she tried to shake him but his laboured breath told her that he was unconscious. They must have drugged him, no wonder that he'd looked and sounded awful in the study. What was she going to do, because she couldn't leave him here for the whole night? What if some animal came and harmed him? Touching his still form made her realise that he didn't have anything warm on and would soon freeze to death.

"Dear Lord, please don't let it snow." She thought of staying with him until morning but they would both die of exposure to the cold so there was only one thing left for her to do. Go back to the manor and get Sephora and Kate to help her carry the duke out of this place and to safety.

6

THE DARING RESCUE

"Why are we doing this?" Kate mumbled as she followed Tilda and Sephora down the tunnels. "Why am I walking in the cold and in this darkness."

"Sh!" Sephora hissed. "Miss Johnson needs our help so stop whining and let's go."

Kate mumbled something but then fell silent and did as bid. Tilda hurried, knowing that time was of the essence if they were to save the duke's life. "We're here, girl," she thanked God for having given her a keen sense of direction. She rarely ever got lost and only needed to use a road or visit a place once. The second time was always easy for her to trace the place.

The duke was lying exactly where she'd left him and she pulled a small tinderbox from under her cloak. She also had a candle which she quickly lit.

"What?" Kate stared at the prostrate form in shock.

"We have to hurry because getting the duke back to the house will be quite a struggle and we don't want those wicked men to catch us."

"What wicked men?" Sephora asked, looking around fearfully as if expecting someone to jump out of the shadows.

"The men who abducted the duke. Quick, slip these two pieces of wood into the frock," Tilda instructed and watched as the two young ladies did it. "Now, let's get the duke onto that stretcher. It's not the best form of conveyance but it'll have to do for now."

The duke was a heavy man and the three women were huffing by the time they managed to roll him onto their contraption. "Sephora and I will pull from the front while Kate, you make sure your uncle doesn't get hurt any more than necessary."

"Yes, Miss Johnson."

Getting the duke back to the manor was harder than she'd expected and Tilda even thought of abandoning their plan. But his life was in danger and she knew that she would do anything for this man because she loved him. It was foolishness on her part but she didn't care, she loved Abel Wickham, the Duke of Nottingham. That gave her the strength to bring him to safety and when they finally entered their rooms, the three women collapsed in fatigue.

"Miss Johnson," Sephora observed after a while. "Only a woman in love could do something as stupid as you just did."

Tilda went red and was glad that the candles in their rooms weren't as bright as those used by the duke for the rest of the house. She had picked one candle made of beeswax and thought of lighting it but then changed her mind. The ones made of tallow were what servants had access to and she could get into trouble if found with the better kind.

"Sephora, that's not a nice thing to say about Miss Johnson," Kate protested, as she got to her feet. "May I please go to sleep now?"

"We can't leave the duke in this open room where anyone can come in and find him. Imagine the kind of trouble we'll be in should someone walk in and find Lord Wickham lying unconscious in our rooms. Girls, help me get him to the inner room and onto the bed. Once he's well rested, I'm sure he'll wake up."

"Or we could use smelling salts to get him to wake up."

"Much as that idea appeals to me, Sephora, we also need our rest. Now, we'll take it in turns to sleep and watch over the duke, just in case someone tries to come into our rooms."

"Yes, Miss Johnson." Sephora insisted on taking the first watch. She would wake Kate after two hours and then Kate would wake Tilda for the early morning shift.

When Tilda was woken up, it was around three a.m. and she went to the kitchen to stir up the fire and get the water in the large cauldron heated. The male servants, bless their souls, would come and fetch the water for the guests who were awake early enough to take their baths. Tilda promised herself that after these festivities were over, she would never put herself in the position of being a domestic servant again. It was too much work and very little rest.

The colour had returned to the duke's face and he was breathing easier now. As she sat on the rickety chair beside the bed, she looked into the face of the man she loved and sighed.

He was a duke, for crying out loud, and she nothing but a lowly servant. Their lives were worlds apart and at his age and with his position, he was probably betrothed to some woman. Tilda felt jealous at the thought of another woman being with Abel, holding his hand, lying beside him and bearing his children.

"Stop being foolish," she silently berated herself. "This man would never spare you a single glance. Get it in your head that you're paths will never meet other than as master and servant."

"Sh! He's stirring."

"Stop making so much noise."

Abel heard the whispers right above his head and opened his eyes. He was disoriented at first.

"Perhaps you shouldn't have overdone the smelling salts."

"Sephora, shut up."

"What's going on here?" Abel blinked rapidly and three scared looking faces came into view. "What are you doing in my bedchamber?"

"This is our room, your grace," Kate said rudely and earned herself a stern look from Tilda.

"Your grace, if you would perhaps sit up and partake of this cup of hot tea, we'll soon explain what has happened."

Tilda's calm and rational words had him nodding. He sat up and received the cup from her hand. It tasted sweet, just what he needed and when he'd gobbled it all down, gave a murmur of appreciation.

"Am I to take it that you've kidnapped me and are hoping to force my hand into doing what you want?"

"Miss Johnson, I told you he wouldn't think any better of us once he woke up."

"Will you just stop, Kate? Actually, go into the kitchen and make sure the ham isn't getting overcooked. Now, young lady!"

Kate left grumbling and Sephora followed soon after. Tilda turned to Abel. "Your grace, do you remember anything at all about last night?"

Abel frowned. "The last thing I remember was feeling a blinding headache and you were there in my study."

"Yes, I was to bring you some lemon and honey."

"Then I remember suddenly feeling cold and .." he touched the back of his head. It felt quite tender and he winced. "Someone struck me at the back of my head."

"I found two men dragging you down the tunnels."

Abel stared at her in shock. "Those things still exist? I thought my father had sealed them up years ago when Oliver, Tamara and I would play in them and get into all kinds of mischief."

"Someone must have reopened them to use for whatever sinister activities they were up to. But last night, you were dragged through the tunnels and when I brought your drink back and found you gone, I noticed the panel behind your desk seemed odd. I followed until the men dumped you in a woodcutter's cottage."

"I remember that too. No wonder that I feel black and blue all over."

Tilda smiled sheepishly, "Some of that, I'm afraid, is also our fault when we were bringing you back to the manor. We didn't have a proper stretcher so we had to improvise. I'm sorry."

"Hey," Abel reached out a hand and touched Tilda's cheek, causing her to blush furiously.

"You saved my life, that's all that counts. But for you, I might be lying dead out there from the cold or wild animals or even those animals who took me there in the first place. Thank you so much."

He made as if to get off the bed but she held out a hand. "Where are you going?"

"To find out who would dare lay a hand on me."

"You still need to lie down for a few more minutes. It's clear that you were drugged and I'm sorry that I didn't realise it at the time, otherwise I wouldn't have left you alone in the study."

"It was a good thing you did, because had those wicked men come in and found you, there's no telling what harm might have come upon you."

"I'm just glad that you're fine, your grace."

"You say you followed the men, did they call each other by name?" She shook her head.

"Did you happen to see their faces?" Once again she shook her head. "How do you think we'll identify them?"

"Their voices. If I should hear them speak, I know that I'll be able to identify them."

"Very well then, we'll have everyone assemble in the drawing room and you'll be in the small side room listening in on every conversation. What?" He asked when he saw her shaking her head.

"For someone to know about the tunnels means they belong to this household, or are close to someone who does. This was clearly the work of someone well known to you. It could be the servants, or any relatives and friends. But these men were determined to get rid of you by whatever means necessary."

"What do you suggest that I do?"

"Do you trust all your servants?" This was from Kate, who'd just returned to the room.

"There are those who've been with the family for long, those I can trust with my life. However, a number are also quite new and are yet to earn my trust. What do you have in mind?" he looked from one woman to the other.

"Which particular servants do you trust most?" Tilda nodded at Kate in approval.

"Gerald Brinks the butler and Peter Reed, the chief stableman. Oh yes, and a couple more but those are ill with the flu."

"Or could have used that as an excuse to make their wicked plans. We have to eliminate the trusted servants and I suggest that Sephora find them and bring them to the kitchen. Gerald may not speak much but I highly doubt that he was one of those two. But I'll listen to him in any case and rule him out as a culprit." Kate left the room to return to the kitchen.

"My life is in your hands, dear lady. Do what you have to do but I need to rid my manor of vermin today. After serving everyone lunch, I'm going to insist that they take their leave and this is the last party of this kind that I'll ever throw. I've been very careless with my life, and my father used to warn me that as a duke, I have to watch my back all the time."

"I'm sorry about all this," Tilda didn't want to imagine how the poor man must be feeling; betrayed by his own. "I'll get to it now."

7

EXPOSING THE WICKED

Once Gerald and Peter had been ruled out as the culprits behind the plot to harm the duke, Kate led them into the servants' room. Their eyes widened when they found their master reclining on the old couch.

"Now Gerald, before you go demanding answers from these fair ladies, just listen to what they have to say." Abel nodded at Tilda, who quickly gave them a rundown of what had happened.

"Who dared do such a wicked thing to my duke," Gerald looked really angry and Tilda feared for the wicked men. This man, regal and formal as he was, looked like he could do someone harm for trying to hurt his master. "I'll deal with them in a way that they'll be sorry all their lives."

"Gerald, please calm down. We still have to catch those men but I promise, I'll let you box their ears," Abel winked at Tilda who hid a smile.

"What if you return to the woodcutter's hut and let those men find you, while Gerald and Peter hide in wait?" Tilda didn't like the plan much but what else could they do?

"Or better still," Abel sat up. "Peter, run down to the village and get the constable as well as my solicitor. Have them come here so I can tell them what's going on and we can then set a trap for those men."

"Yes, your lordship."

While Peter went to do as bid, Gerald took over the women's quarters temporarily and helped the duke to clean up. He also stood watch as his master partook of a hearty meal and then remained watching as he took a nap. It was still quite dark outside and he hoped Peter would hurry up and return. The presence of the constable in the house would be reassuring.

"You ladies deserve so much more than just praise," Gerald stepped into the kitchen briefly to thank the three women for what they had done. "When his grace is better, you can be sure that he'll reward you."

Tilda smiled at the butler, who seemed so much friendlier now. "We're just happy that the duke is alright."

"I have to get back and watch our master. This has been a very shocking discovery."

"It will soon be over and life will return to normal," Tilda said. As she spoke the words out loud, realised their implication and sighed.

It meant that her work would soon be over at the manor and they would be bid farewell and expected to return to their ordinary world.

"It's been an exciting few hours but this food won't serve itself, Tilda," Sephora had a sardonic look on her face. "We need to lay out the table before someone from above begins shouting for their food."

"You're right," Tilda agreed. "Let's make sure the guests are all taken care of because we don't want them finding out what is going on."

"Gerald and the other male servants can help us out. The sooner all this is over, the sooner we can go back to our lives," Kate said, biting her bottom lip.

Tilda felt sorry for the younger lady "I'm sorry you expected to find your uncle and that he would acknowledge you. Still, we'll at least leave this place with a little money and I know the orphanage could do with some helpers."

"That's the last place I want to be in."

"You have no choice, Sephora. Until something better comes up, that's where we'll go when we leave this place."

"Why don't you marry the duke," the younger woman blurted out.

"Sephora."

"Miss Johnson, I see the way you look at my uncle and he you. I just wish the two of you would realise that you have feelings for each other."

"Kate, I would expect that from Sephora, not you."

"But it's the truth..."

"Shush! I won't have you talking about things you have no understanding of. Let's do what we're supposed to and hope that the duke will be alright."

Abel had just stepped off the couch and wanted to stretch his legs when he heard the three women in the kitchen. What they didn't know was that though they were trying to whisper, their voices carried. He smiled at the panic in Tilda's voice. Clearly, her two younger companions had seen what she wasn't aware of or perhaps she was but was trying to hide it. In any case, his own problem was bigger. He was in love with Matilda and then there was someone after his life. He really wondered who it was.

Peter returned after half an hour with the village constable and Abel's private solicitor. The visitors were quickly filled in on what was going on, and after a light meal, the four men escorted Abel back to the woodcutter's hut. Dawn was just breaking but the thick bushes were good enough to conceal the four men.

Clearly no one had been by so the four men took positions outside to see who would come in and try to harm the duke. Abel sat on the floor of the hut wondering why he hadn't had it pulled down some time ago. Someone might be using it as a den where vile men meet, and that would also mean it was a security risk for his manor. Being out here, who knows what people might plot and come up with?

They waited for a while but no one seemed to be coming. Abel began to wonder if Tilda hadn't imagined the whole thing, but how then did he end up in the servants' quarters? He somehow couldn't see Tilda dragging him through the corridors of the manor all alone. But wait, she had her two friends with her and they were determined that he would acknowledge Kate as his sister's daughter. But he didn't have a sister, unless he asked one of the longest serving servants. Gerald Brinks might have an answer but before he could open his mouth to call out to his servant, he heard heavy footsteps.

So he lay down and pretended to be sleeping "See, I told you he'd still be here."

"I was just worried that the servants might find him and take him away."

"Those good for nothing idiots are too full of themselves to be of any use to their lord. Now I'll finish him off and we'll see what they will do. The moment this idiot is gone, I'm sacking all the oldies and getting rid of the useless crowd. Things are going to change around here."

Abel couldn't believe that it was his cousin Oliver who was behind the plot to harm him. It shocked and saddened him because all he'd ever wanted was for his relatives to be happy. Apparently all they wanted was for him to be gone so they could take over the duchy. His inner sorrow made him groan.

"Did he say something?" Luke asked in a fearful voice.

"He's still drugged, probably just turning in his dreams," Oliver said with a laugh. "If you can't watch me doing this, please leave the hut. I'll let you know when it's all over."

"Why don't we just abandon the duke somewhere instead of you killing him? After all, he's your close relative."

"I'm getting rather tired of your whining and childishness, Luke. Of course, when the duke just disappears, all eyes will turn on me. He could then return and knowing my cousin, will begin searching for whoever caused his disappearance. Think of how that will go, Luke. If he's dead and no one knows what kills him, they will be concentrating on finding his killers and sympathizing with me."

"I can't bear to watch."

"Whether you stay or leave, if this ever gets out, we're both going to hang. You might as well help me finish this off."

Abel opened his eyes just as his cousin was about to lower the stick over his head. "Why not just shoot me, Oliver," he said in a dry voice. "That will save you the mess of cleaning up afterwards."

"Too noisy. I….you're awake!'

"Indeed, go ahead and finish what you started seeing as I now know who is behind the plot to kill me. Of all the people, Oliver, you're the last person I would have thought wanted me dead. Tamara maybe and a few other cousins, but never you."

"Just shut up and close your eyes. It will be less painful that way."

"You do what you have to do, but let my eyes ever follow you wherever you go from now on."

"Aargh!" Oliver cried out in frustration and once again raised the stick.

"You'll be dead before that stick descends," the cold voice came from the door and Oliver saw the constable pointing two pistols at him. "Step away from Lord Wickham this instant, or so help me, I'll shoot you in the head and stomach at the same time."

When Gerald and Peter saw that Oliver was slow to do as bid, they rushed him, while Abel's solicitor tackled the cowering Luke.

Once the men were overpowered and bound securely, Abel sat up and turned his intense gaze on Luke. He knew that was the weaker man who would likely give him the information he sought.

"Why Luke?"

"It was all Oliver's idea."

"Shut up, Luke."

"He wanted to be duke because of his debts. You've been paying them off but he wants to control the purse strings himself. That was why he came up with the idea of killing you."

"You're both going to hang," the constable said, as he motioned for the solicitor to help him lead the two men away. They left and Gerald helped his master to his feet.

"We need to get you home at once, your grace."

"Thank you both for your help in all this. I just want to go back home to a peaceful environment without all the noise of revelers."

"Have no fear, Miss Johnson assured me that by the time we returned, most guests will have left and the remaining few will be very quiet. Very diplomatic but efficient lady," Gerald gave Abel a look which he chose to ignore.

"Very well then, shall we be on our way?"

8

THE HIDDEN TRUTH

It was good to be back home again, and this time to a quiet manor. It seemed like the party hadn't even taken place because everything was back in its rightful place and the carriages that had lined up the driveway for miles were all gone.

Only one or two guests still remained, but those could easily be handled. Abel stretched himself out on the chaise longue in his study, an indulgence he rarely allowed himself. His whole body was sore from all the dragging that had been done, but he was alive and well, thanks to Tilda Johnson and her two friends.

He rang the bell and Gerald was in the room at once. "You called, your grace?"

"Get off your feet for a brief moment, my good man." He looked at his butler who made no move to sit down. It just wasn't proper, according to Gerald and Abel knew that the man would never sit in his presence. "Well, you can continue standing if you so wish."

"Thank you, my lord."

"Gerald, tell me something. What do you know about me having a sister?"

Gerald observed his master for a while and then sighed. "It was so long ago that I'd all but forgotten, forgive me, your grace."

"It's alright. What can you tell me?"

"My lord, the late Duke of Nottingham took a wife when he was just about eighteen and the lass was sixteen. It was an arranged marriage but from the onset, the poor lass didn't seem to want to belong to this family. She died as she was putting to bed, bringing forth a baby girl."

Abel sat up straight. "Where's that child?"

"My lady's elder sister was visiting when the child was born. As soon as the duchess was buried, she left with the child and we never heard of her again. Over the years, before your father, the duke, married your mother, he tried to find his daughter and even gave up, thinking that she might have died."

Abel sat with his head bowed.

"Your grace, I'm sorry to give you such distressing news."

"It's not your fault, could you get me Miss Johnson and the other two young ladies, please?"

"Yes, your grace."

As Abel waited for the women to join him in his study, he found himself unable to sit still. What if Kate was really the daughter of his long lost sister? So it was true that he had a sister of whom he had no knowledge, but what had happened to her and why wasn't his father unable to trace the whereabouts of the child?

There was a soft knock at the door. "Please come in." Abel waited for the three women to file into his study. "Please take a seat." But like Gerald, they chose to stand. "I've been speaking to Gerald about the past and he told me something very interesting." The women just looked at him without saying a word. "It's true that my father had another child, a girl, so yes, I had an elder sister but according to Gerald, my father wasn't able to trace her whereabouts when she left here as an infant."

Gerald nodded, "The duke was so distraught at losing his young wife and child, and he did all he could to find out where the duchess's sister had gone. For many years, the duke didn't take a wife again because he always expected to find his daughter. But finally, after about fifteen years, he met my lord's mother. By that time, no one spoke about the missing child and we soon put it out of our minds altogether until a few moments ago when his lordship asked me. That's when I remembered."

Abel was watching Kathleen Crammer as his butler spoke and noticed her twirling a medallion between her fingers. It looked very familiar. "What's that in your hand, Kate?"

Kate held up the medallion. "Mama gave me this when she was very sick. She said it was the only thing of her father's that she had remaining."

Abel reached out his hand. "May I please have a look at it?"

"Sure," Kate handed it over, looking at Tilda with a puzzled expression on her face. Tilda simply shrugged.

They were surprised when Abel reached for the chain around his neck and pulled it off. "This was given to me by my father, and they're so similar. My father used to tell me to find the missing piece, this one's twin and I always assumed that a servant had stolen it from the house."

Gerald's stiff demeanor cracked and he seemed almost excited. "That, your grace, is the family medallion given by the duke to his children at birth. He once told me that it represents the continuity of the family line, that the Wickham lineage will never end. That was the reason he gave it to your sister, so she would one day return home." He looked at Kate. "No wonder I always thought that you reminded me of someone, the duke's cousin, Tamara. I wish your mother had returned home."

"But she has," he looked at Kate and opened his arms. She hesitated briefly then Tilda nudged her gently and she ran to her uncle. "I'm so sorry for doubting you, my dear niece. Welcome to your grandfather's home. I just wish I had known about your mother before, then I would have left no stone unturned in my search for her."

"Uncle Abel," Kate was so overwhelmed that she was shedding tears.

"Don't cry. This is your home now and forever and you will be taken good care of. I'm so sorry for making you into a servant in your own grandfather's home."

"Uncle, that had to be done. Besides, if you hadn't give us the jobs that we had, then we would never have discovered that someone wanted you dead. Who was it now?" Kate had a fierce look on her face. "Who dared to try and harm my uncle, the duke?"

Abel laughed and patted her gently on the shoulder. "Child, it's all been taken care of and the culprits will no longer trouble this family."

"Will they hang?"

"Kate!" Tilda's tone was scandalized.

"She's a true Wickham by blood," Abel said. "Our family were strong defenders of the crown for centuries and that's why one of our ancestors was given the duchy. Otherwise, we were just an ordinary family of soldiers."

"Sounds like a rich history."

"I'll have one of the servants dig up the annals of history then we can get it right. To me it was just a story told at my father and mother's feet, but I think I'll take a closer look now."

"Thank you for all this, your grace," Tilda curtsied. "Allow us to go and serve Christmas lunch now." When Kate made as if to follow them, Tilda curtsied to her as well. "My lady, your uncle and you probably have a lot to discuss. Please allow us to be your servants."

"Miss Johnson," Kate protested but her uncle shook his head slightly and she let them go.

9
BEHOLD THE DUCHESS

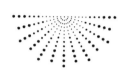

Lunch was over and Abel felt sad that Tilda had refused to join him and Kate. He knew it was all for propriety's sake but more than ever, he wanted her close by his side.

"Kate?"

"Your grace?"

"I'm your uncle and it would give me pleasure to have you address me as such."

"Thank you, uncle. Did you need something?"

"Yes. Would you so kindly ask Miss Johnson to see me in the study?"

"Yes, Uncle." Kate stood up from the dining table to do as bid. At the doorway she stopped and turned around. "Uncle Abel?"

"Yes, my dear niece?"

"Miss Johnson is a wonderful woman and it would be a pity to let titles and social status get in the way of true love," and she left the room before her uncle could say anything else.

Abel chuckled softly, he was going to have to find a governess for his sister's daughter. Kate was delightful and lovely but it was obvious that she'd been brought up to speak her mind, and noble ladies didn't do that, not if they wanted to be socially accepted. Then he stopped himself. Hadn't she just gently chided him about titles and social status? Besides, his relatives had all been brought up by governesses and learning the right way to behave. Yet most of them behaved worse than the commoners.

He shook his head. He wasn't going to impose any regulations on his niece, let her find her own way. He also knew that Matilda Johnson was the best guide that Kate needed and he was going to see that she stayed. Picking up his stick for he needed one for a few days, he went to the study to await her arrival.

Tilda didn't know why she felt so nervous as she stood in front of the study door. She could hear Abel moving about and taking a deep breath, she knocked.

"Well, here goes nothing," she murmured as she opened the door when bid to enter. "Your grace," she curtsied. "Lady Kate said that you wanted to see me."

"Please do come in and shut the door," Abel stood behind the desk and observed Tilda. She seemed nervous and he felt comforted somehow. He was also a wreck inside because he didn't know what her response would be to his question. "For once, please sit down in my presence. There's no one else here so we don't have to observe such strict protocol."

"Thank you," Tilda was glad to sit because her legs were shaking so much.

"Matilda, or Tilda as I have heard the girls calling you."

"Your grace."

"My name is Abel and I'd like you to use it," he held up his hand. "Before you go protesting too much, just think about this. Which wife calls her husband by his title in the privacy of their chambers when they're all alone?"

Tilda was confused. "I don't understand."

"You do, my dear," Abel said softly and approached her. He sat down on the chair opposite hers and took her hands. "I don't like beating around the bush so I'll just say what's in my heart. From the moment you stood at my doorstep, I fell in love with you, Matilda Johnson. That was the reason that I decided to keep you around, so you could find out the kind of man that I am, then I would ask you to be my wife, my duchess."

"What?" Tilda thought she was dreaming. How could this noble and handsome man be declaring his love for her? Was this some kind of a joke?

"Tilda," he rubbed the backs of her hands with his thumbs. "You're everything that a man would desire in a wife. Beautiful, mature, bold, courageous and very loving. For centuries, the Wickham men have married wives not based on their titles or social standing, but on their personal and individual character. Gerald has told me so many times that you remind him of my mother, that noble woman. He knew her before I was born and even after, and she was well loved not just by her family, but servants and tenants as well."

"I don't know what to say, your grace."

"Abel."

"Abel." Tilda said the name softly and she heard him grunt in satisfaction.

"There, it sounds so beautiful on your lips." He raised her hands and kissed both of them gently. "Tilda, I know that it's only been two days since you came into my life, but it feels like I've known you for a lifetime. This duchy needs a duchess such as yourself and that's why I'm going to be so bold as to ask you to be my wife, even though I'm shaking inside."

"Oh Abel," Tilda could see the vulnerability in his eyes and felt touched at his confession. Yes, this was the right kind of man, one who knew that he was strong and yet wasn't afraid to admit his fears also. He was just the kind of man she'd been praying for.

"I know that you don't have feelings for me, yet, but I promise to be a good husband, one who will take care of you and Sephora. I used to laugh at friends and acquaintances when they claimed to have fallen in love at first sight, but now that it's happened to me, I know it's real." He sighed. "Can you take this man to be your husband, a man who will love you for the rest of his life?"

"Yes, I can," she said softly at first. And really meant it. "Yes, Abel."

"Thank you, and I promise that I'll never ask for more than you can give."

"My love," it was her turn to kiss his hands. "I love you but never thought this could be possible. When I thought that someone wanted to hurt you," her eyes clouded over.

"Darling, it's all over."

"I wanted to tear those men from limb to limb. It's a good thing I didn't immediately know who they were or there would have been trouble."

"A true Wickham bride," Abel chuckled. "Our children will learn so much about courage and boldness at your feet, my darling."

"I would really love that."

"Now, we've had an upheaval at the duchy and I'd like to make an announcement and present you to the entire household." He rang the bell to summon Gerald. The old butler's only reaction to their entwined hands was a knowing smile on his normally austere face.

"Your grace?"

"Gather all the servants and guests in the ballroom for I have a special announcement to make on this special Christmas Day. My life was preserved and the woman I love has agreed to be my wife. Gerald, behold your new duchess."

Gerald curtsied, and left the room to do as bid.

THANK YOU FOR CHOOSING A PUREREAD BOOK!

We hope you enjoyed the story, and as a way to thank you for choosing PureRead we'd like to send you this free book, and other fun reader rewards...

An undercover plan designed to win a young nobleman's heart is threatened when the lovely Gabrielle Belgrade's soft conscience and honesty threatens to undo the matchmaking shenanigans of Lord Grant's well intentioned godmother.

Click here for your free copy of The Pretender
PureRead.com/regency

Thanks again for reading.
See you soon!

OUR GIFT TO YOU

AS A WAY TO SAY THANK YOU WE WOULD LOVE TO SEND YOU THIS BEAUTIFUL STORY FREE OF CHARGE.

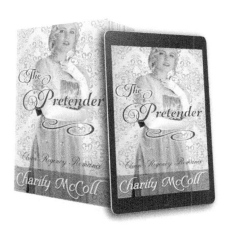

An undercover plan designed to win a young nobleman's heart is threatened when the lovely Gabrielle Belgrade's soft conscience and honesty threatens to undo the matchmaking shenanigans of Lord Grant's well intentioned godmother.

Click here for your free copy of The Pretender

PureRead.com/regency

At PureRead we publish books you can trust. Great tales without smut or swearing, but with all of the mystery and romance you expect from a great story.

Be the first to know when we release new books, take part in our fun competitions, and get surprise free books in your inbox by signing up to our free VIP Reader list.

As a thank you you'll receive a copy of *The Pretender* straight away in you inbox.

Click here for your free copy of The Pretender

PureRead.com/regency

Printed in Great Britain
by Amazon

42286206R00067